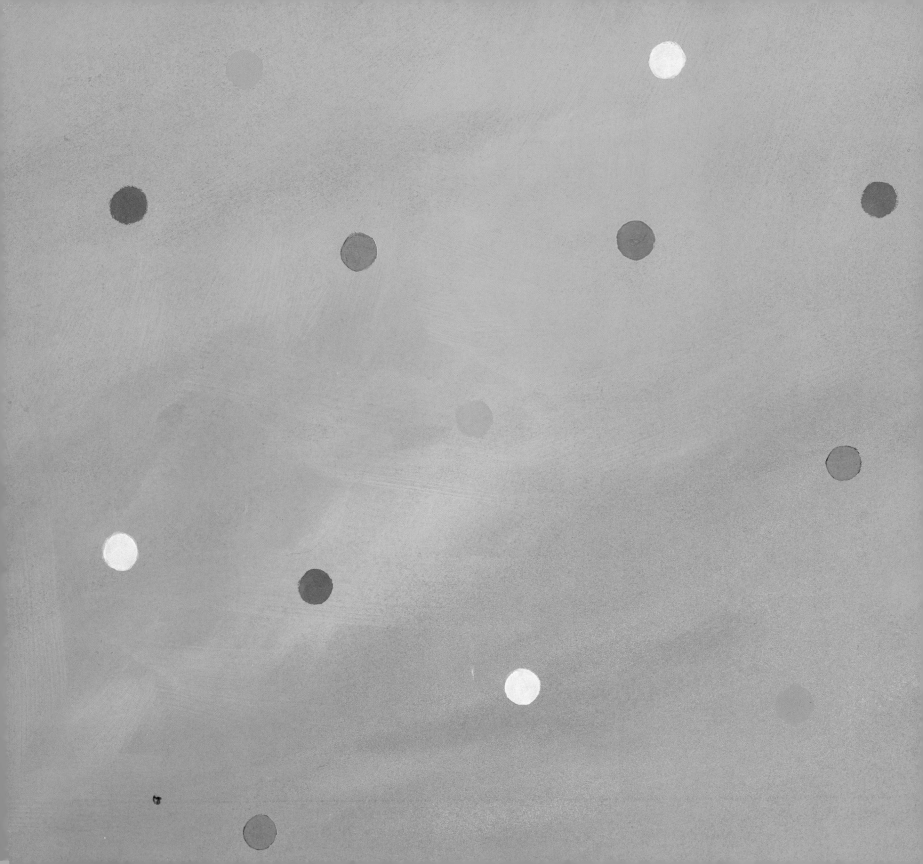

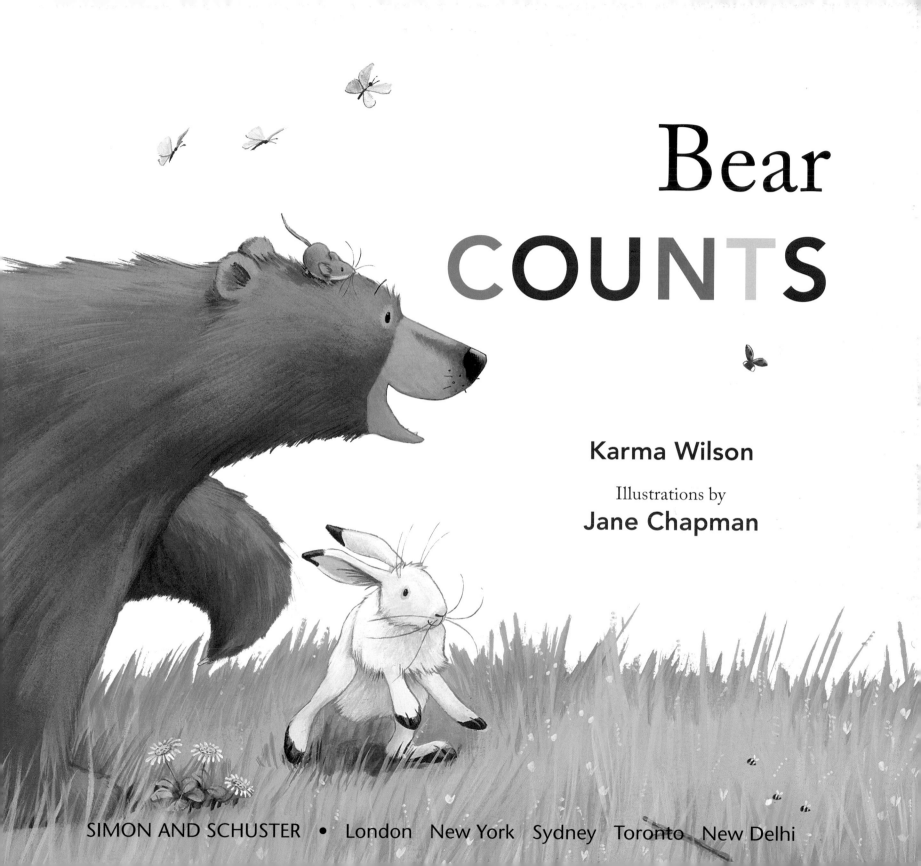

Bear
COUNTS

Karma Wilson

Illustrations by
Jane Chapman

SIMON AND SCHUSTER • London New York Sydney Toronto New Delhi

Mouse and Bear share breakfast,
basking in the morning sun.
Bear looks up and points,
and the bear

counts . . .

one!

One sun floating high.

One giant dragonfly.

One robin on her nest.
Only ONE berry left!

Numbers, numbers everywhere.
Can you count along with Bear?

1!

Mouse and Bear see Hare,
and Hare calls out, "Howdy do?"
He is holding yummy fruit,
and the bear
counts . . .

two!

Two paws which hold a treat.
Two apples crisp and sweet!

Two stumps for perfect chairs.
Two friends who love to share.

Numbers, numbers everywhere.
Can you count along with Bear?

1,2!

Bear hears funny sounds
coming from an aspen tree.
It is Raven, Owl and Wren,
and the bear
counts . . .

three!

Three chums who chitter-chat.
Three funny muskrats.

Three clouds above the trees.

Three bumbling bumblebees.

Numbers, numbers everywhere.
Can you count along with Bear?

1,2,3!

Bear cries, "Look, it's Badger,
Mole and Gopher by the shore!
Badger has his fishin' pole."
And the bear

counts . . .

four!

Four fish splish 'n' splash.

Four geese waddle past.

Four turtles on a log.

Four croaking, hopping frogs!

Numbers, numbers everywhere.
Can you count along with Bear?

1,2,3,4!

Mouse squeaks, "Let's go swimming!"
And in the pond they dive.
The friends float in the pond.
And the bear
counts . . .

five!

Five ducks in the water.

Five lively river otters.

Five lovely lily pads.

Five pinching crawdads.

Numbers, numbers everywhere.
Now YOU can count, just like BEAR!

1!

2!

3!

One, two, three gorgeous kids! Can you count with Karma?
To Sarah, Nathan, David Brian, Atticus Daniel,
and Louisa Belle. All my love!
—K. W.

To Dylan, Jacob, and Bump
—J. C.

SIMON AND SCHUSTER • First published in Great Britain in 2015 by Simon and Schuster UK Ltd • 1st Floor, 222 Gray's Inn Road, London WC1X 8HB • A CBS company • Originally published by Margaret K. McElderry Books, an imprint of Simon and Schuster Children's Publishing Division, New York • Text copyright © 2015 Karma Wilson • Illustrations copyright © 2015 Jane Chapman • The right of Karma Wilson and Jane Chapman to be identified as the author and illustrator of this work has been asserted by them in accordance with the Copyright, Designs and Patents Act, 1988 • All rights reserved, including the right of reproduction in whole or in part in any form • A CIP catalogue record for this book is available from the British Library upon request • ISBN: 978-1-4711-2545-4 • Printed in China • 10 9 8 7 6 5 4 3 2 1 • www.simonandschuster.co.uk

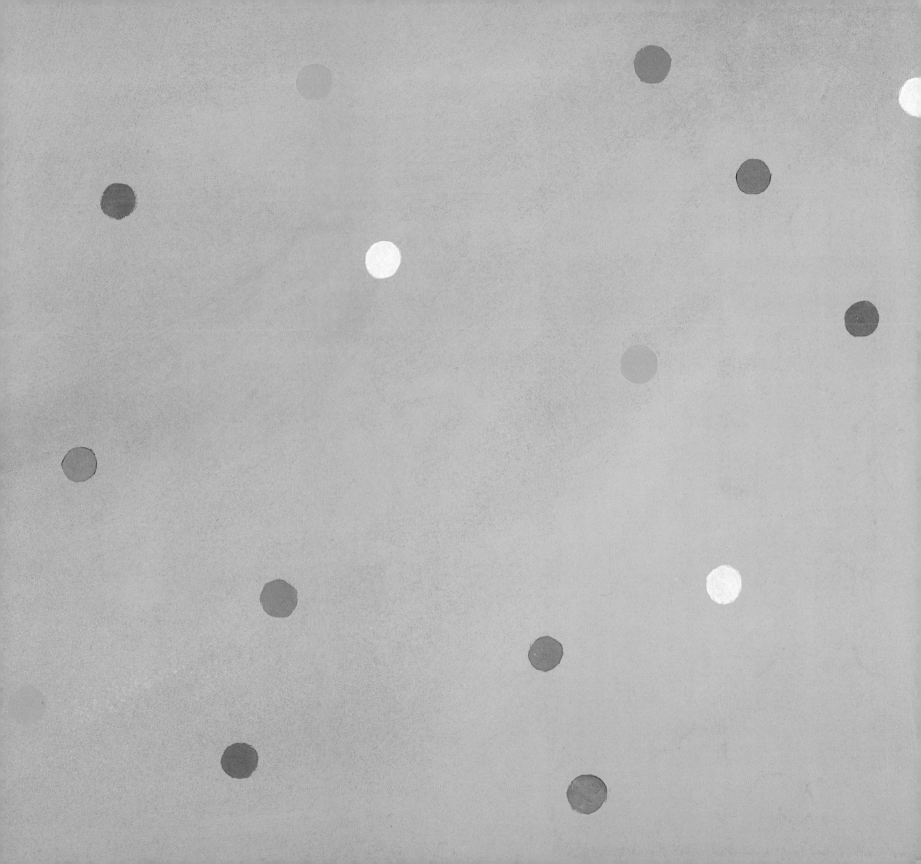